THE RIGHT ANGLE CLUB

Annual Report 2014

Copyright 2014

Printed by Ross & Perry, Inc., 2014

© Ross & Perry, Inc., 2014 on new material. All Rights reserved.

Printed in the United States of America

Ross & Perry, Inc. Publishers
3 South Haddon Avenue, Suite 4
Haddonfield, N.J. 08033
Telephone (856) 427-6135
Facsimile (856) 427-6136
Visit us at www.rossperry.com
http://www.rossperry.com

ISBN: 978-1-932109-51-1

Book Cover designed by Just Ink

Table of Contents

To see photos in color visit http://www.philadelphia-reflections.com/topic/247.htm

TOPIC 247 Right Angle Club: 2014

BLOG 2761 President's Letter 5

BLOG 2730 Our President Shows His Stuff 6

BLOG 2746 Talkie Revolution 7

BLOG 2728 At Times, Charles Dickens was a Little Immature 8

BLOG 2662 What' a Ribosome? Who is Joachim Frank? 10

BLOG 2677 Decline and Fall of Philadelphia 11

BLOG 2669 All Right, Hippocrates. So What's the Basic Problem? 14

BLOG 1696 Cost Shifting: Indigent Care Out, Outpatient Revenue, In 18

BLOG 2655 Indemnity and Payment by Diagnosis: Fair Prices for Healthcare 20

BLOG 2649 American Exceptionalism has Something to Do With Compromise 21

Poetry by Tom Howes (continued on pg 43) 24

BLOG 2659 Enforcing the Constitution: Civil Monetary Penalties (CMP) 29

BLOG 2658 Philadelphia's Real Estate Gridlock 30

BLOG 2264 Too Much Money 33

BLOG 2660 Arbitration 35

BLOG 2663 Honoring the Fallen 36

BLOG 2667 The Last of the Algonquins 38

BLOG 2642 James F. Kilcur, Esq. 39

BLOG 2759 Dr. F. Douglas Raymond, Jr. 41

BLOG 2760 Neale C. Bringhurst. 42

Poetry by Tom Howes (continued from pg 28) 43

BLOG 2762 Our Jokester has Another Side to Him. 48

Right Angle Club 2014

Still the Right Angle, after 92 years.

President's Letter for 2014

David J Richards MD

Well, the 92nd year of the Right Angle Club is coming to an end. It has been successful in many ways.

How to describe this eventful time. In a word it was consolidation, to build up a solid base from which we can keep up the high quality of club offerings of weekly speakers, flings, good food and camaraderie at a reasonable price. With this foundation we can communicate with enthusiasm the virtues that our club has to offer to prospective members.

It is a continual amazement that our club is consistently able to provide, year after year, a cadre of about 42 speakers on a wide range of topics with good quality of food, together with three social events where significant others are invited, as well as our renowned President's Dinner. All of this provided at a very reasonable cost. I know of no other similar club that provides such value.

This high standard can only be kept by the hard work of the club's Board of Control. The First Vice President, Carter Broach, has always been available in the inevitable crises that occur. He has even solved the perennial tie problem. Wayne Strasburgh has presented us with three great flings The Sedgeley Club on the Schuykill River, Waynesborough in Chester County, and most recently the spectacular Christmas event at the Acorn Club, the oldest female club in the USA. Dan Sossaman II provided us with a stimulating series of speakers as well as meetings which stretched the member's knowledge of Philadelphia. Chad Bardone conducted the raffle with the efficiency of a tax collector. The results of his efforts will be sent to our charity, The Philadelphia Scholarship fund.

All of the above could only be accomplished with the monies from our dues . Our accounts are most effectually administered by our Treasurer, Thomas Williams, who continues to amaze with the complexity of the reports he produces at each Board of Control meeting. Mel Buckman remains our admirable recording secretary who keeps our memory in order and Dan Sossaman Sr. who ably served as Chairman of the Nominating committee. The members at large of your Board of Control, Peter Alois, Steve Bennet, JohnCoates and Jack Foltz, provided sage advice on all topics. We are also blessed with the invaluable services of LeAnne Lindsey who now acts as the focus of our clubs contact with its members with all things we need to know through Constant Contact.

On the consolidation front, we have obtained a firm footing financially which enables us to predict with reasonable degree of confidence our future income and expenditures based upon on our current and future projected membership.

With our lecture series, lunches, friendship and events coupled with a stable financial situation we are in a good position to attract new members to our club.

We are fortunate to have, subject to approval at our annual general meeting, an outstanding slate of new officers to serve for what I am certain will be a great 93rd year for Right Angle Club.

Your most obedient servant

David J Richards MD 92nd President 17 December 2014

http://www.philadelphia-reflections.com/blog/2761.htm

Our President Shows His Stuff

Three of our members recently flew to Argentina to play Rugby. That was Jack Nixon, John Wetzel, and our President, David Richards. We have all grown a little tired of being told that football is for sissies; Rugby, now that's a real man's sport. Down there, South of the Border, they really know how to play soccer, so Rugby is a natural for the Argentines. Well, eventually they came back, and we discover that our President was awarded a medal. John said it took him twenty years to win a medal, but Richards won it the first time he tried.

Rugby

President David Richards

Since he was at the microphone, President David had no choice but to tell us how it happened. It seems the new team had uniform pants which were a couple inches shorter than his underwear, so in desperation he decided to play without any underwear. At one moment crucial to the game, he was holding the ball, but the Argentine tackled him by grabbing the pants-top from behind. And so our hero was standing there pantless, holding the ball. So he was faced with an awful choice: either he must let down the team, or else run for the goal, dressed (or undressed) as he was.

So, of course he ran for the goal. The bleachers went wild, cellphones clicked themselves silly, and our hero made the goal. And naturally, the Argentines respected excellence, so they gave him a medal.

http://www.philadelphia-reflections.com/blog/2730.htm

Talkie Revolution

George Strimel dropped by the Right Angle Club recently, showing us a marvelous video of the era which ended in October, 1927. It's fast fading into the past, and others remember 1929 as a more memorable date. Some have heard of the roaring Twenties, prohibition, repeal, and Bobby Jones the golfer. But in entertainment circles, the end of the silent films is more celebrated as the turning point that matters. Why so? Why is the end of dark, flickering, silent movies such a big deal?

George Strimel, who has spent his life in public broadcasting, made it all come clear, while hardly saying a word. He just played his video.

George Strimel

George is one of the survivors of the roaring twenties, and something of a venerated figure among those who care about silent films. There is quite a group who feel that silent films required more money, talent, and effort to produce than either vaudeville, which they replaced, or "talkies" which in their opinion undeservedly vanquished them at the box office. For one thing, there was a strong European presence among the opinion makers, bringing along memories of the recent "Great" war and the great awakening of Americans to modern European culture. We particularly favored British films, of course, but not

Greta Garbo

because of their upper-class accents. They were part of the European conquest of American culture, along with Germans, Hungarians, French and Italians. But as soon as talkies exposed their foreign accents, it was mainly the English who survived in the American market. Do you remember Cary Grant, Guy Kibbee, Basil Rathbone, and Mary Astor? The movie moguls, ever watchful for a profit, were very hesitant at first about Greta Garbo and Claudette Colbert.

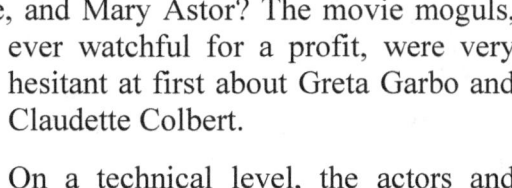

On a technical level, the actors and actresses found it difficult to function without whispered stage directions from the directors. It was harder, you had to memorize more, and consequently it was more expensive to produce a talkie than a silent film. More than half of the artistic effect of silent films actually came from the dubbed-in background music, which told the

Al Jolson

audience they were approaching a tender moment, or a stirring battle scene. The musical director began to play a much diminished role in the product, and the actors really had to act out the meaning of a scene.

And let's not forget the musicians who played live music in the gigantic movie palaces. At the time Al Jolson was performing in the Jazz Singer, there were over 22,000 union musicians who were about to be thrown permanently out of work. Philadelphia had the Erlanger, the Mastbaum and the Boyd, as well as a dozen smaller movie palaces who turned the theater musicians out of work, and then slowly died out, themselves. Coming in to Philadelphia on the trolleys was the thing to do with your evenings for another decade or two, but the writing was on the wall. The center of union musicianship was at Broad and Locust for a while; all during the Second World War there was union unrest and some Communist mutterings, centered in the old Adelphia Hotel. It was natural to blame that on the Academy of Music across the street, but unemployed movie theater musicians were a part of it, too.

Most of us think of that era in terms of World War II, the Great Depression, the 1929 Stock Market Crash, and other momentous events in history. But to some people, the turning point of our whole culture really began in October 1927, when Al Jolson astounded the world with the Jazz Singer. And nothing in the entertainment world was ever quite the same.

http://www.philadelphia-reflections.com/blog/2746.htm

At Times, Charles Dickens Was a Little Immature

Quaker Origins

Every once in a while, Philadelphia needs to be reminded of its Quaker origins, and the surprising number of people who will suddenly make an appearance to defend Quaker ideas. It would appear that Philadelphia needs to be reminded that Quakers see a value, even a joy, in silence. The present entrepreneurs in charge of Eastern State Penitentiary, presently a Hallowe'en showplace, are to be congratulated for rehabilitating a neighborhood formerly in decay. If you are looking for a collection of exotic restaurants after visiting the neighborhood art museums, this is the place to go. But I do wish somebody would put an end to the myth that silence and solitary confinement can drive you crazy, because I don't believe they will.

Every Quaker family has to handle the problem that children don't naturally like to sit still. The first few times Quaker children are brought to meeting, the kids have to be shushed, given books to read, and eventually be led out early to sit in the First-Day (Sunday school) classrooms, while their parents go back to the meeting room to sit in silence. Some kids get the message quicker than others, and the ones who keep misbehaving in meeting eventually have to face general disapproval as "spoiled" until they either quiet down, or get sent to boarding school. So Quakers are familiar with the problem, learn how to deal with it, and tend to regard resistance to silence as a sign of immaturity.

Charles Dickens

Charles Dickens was once a newspaper reporter in Philadelphia, and wrote many ecstatic articles about the city. However, he was paid by the word, and prospered mightily from some unnecessarily long articles directed to the folks back in England. One of them was a description of Eastern Penitentiary, built on the principle of the rehabilitation of criminal behavior by long periods of solitude, remote from distracting criminal influences in the community at large. The idea, which may well have originated with Dr. Benjamin Rush, later called the father of American Psychiatry, was widely imitated. There soon were over three hundred prisons throughout the world, dedicated to the idea and imitating the architecture. Whether he believed it or not, Dickens wrote a long, long, diatribe against the concept of solitude as rehabilitating, in which he imagined himself in the position of the poor prisoner, and declaring it would drive him crazy. Without much argument, Charles Dickens was responsible for the shift in public attitudes which eventually led the Board of Prisons to decide to tear it down. This was not exactly evidence-based psychiatric reasoning, since a

Dr. Benjamin Rush

great many crazy people get sent to prison anyway. It isn't surprising that lots of crazy people were found in Eastern Penitentiary, but it isn't exactly proven that solitary confinement made them into lunatics. In fact, it isn't being based on evidence to claim that either the outcome of recidivism, or the outcome of improved behavior is influence by any form of incarceration, with or without corporal punishment, with or without capital punishment. It is definitely proven that incarceration is as expensive as psychiatric treatment, but that isn't saying a great deal. You can definitely cause temporary insanity with prolonged sleep deprivation, but you would suppose that solitary confinement would increase the amount of sleep, not reduce it.

When the time came to demolish Eastern Penitentiary, the Board of Prisons was advised it was so solidly constructed it was simply too expensive to tear it down. As the neighborhood gentrified, real estate values rose, but never enough to justify the demolition of what was essentially a fortress. Even the relentless forces of decay have continued to be slower than the rise of rise in price of the land. It's like those medieval castles still standing in Europe, occasionally attracting some American billionaire, but mostly just hollow shells. The deterioration on the interior is apt to go faster than deterioration of those stone walls, so the cells formerly occupied by Willie Sutton and Al Capone will need restoration sooner than the towers and parapets. But driving people crazy? It's doubtful. Its function was mostly to segregate the criminal elements of each succeeding wave of immigrants, as quick review of the surnames of inmates easily demonstrates.

http://www.philadelphia-reflections.com/blog/2728.htm

What's a Ribosome? Who is Joachim Frank?

Joachim Frank

Every year for many years, the Franklin Institute has been picking eminent scientists, and awarding them prizes. It has already selected over eighty awardees before they won Nobel Prizes, searching out talent, not merely fame. Albert Einstein, Thomas A. Edison, Madame Curie, Bill Gates and a host of other famous scientists have been awarded Franklin Institute Prizes, going back longer than the Nobel Prizes themselves for many years. The awards dinners are usually held in the Spring of the year, and the Institute is completely filled with attendees. In fact, for the past few years the seats have been completely sold out before the invitations are in the mail. It's expensive to attend, the food is outstanding, and it's certainly the most prestigious scientific event of the Philadelphia social season. However, there's something you need to know. The awardees give only the briefest of speeches at the dinner; a full presentation of their scientific work is given on a different day, usually the day before the dinner. If you really have scientific aspirations, we expect to see you at the seminar, where the most eminent scientists the Institute can find explain their work in full scientific detail. At the seminars, they show the audience very little mercy, although the cupcakes and coffee are pretty good.

This year, the most astonishing life scientist was Joachim Frank. He's now on the faculty of Columbia University, but he originally comes from Germany, and did most of his scientific work at General Electric in upstate New York. Much or most of that time was spent taking (electron) photographs of a single molecule, the ribosome, at short intervals and from many different angles. You really have to believe in what you are doing, to take 80,000 photographs of a single molecule. But putting them together amounts to constructing a movie, and a movie of one molecule in action tells you a great deal about what the molecule is doing. That's assuming you believe the molecule is moving around doing something, which is an insight

The Franklin Institute Awards

that most of us wouldn't even think of. A ribosome molecule is a rather large one, covered with knobs which are thinly attached to the main molecule. The knobs waggle around on their narrow attachments, more or less in continuous movement because of the "Brownian movements" of the internal atoms. As soon as microscopes got good enough to see molecules this small, it was clear that the electrons jiggle because the cell constituents are internally composed of atoms, but it was never clear what purpose was served by jiggling the atoms.

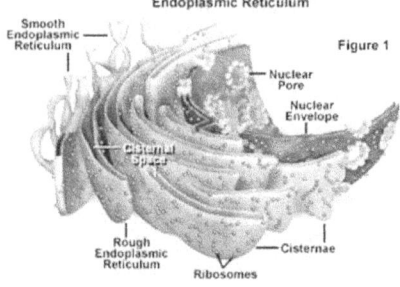

Endoplasmic Reticulum

By watching the synthetic movies derived from photographing the ribosomes, it eventually became clear that the knobs were jiggling on the surface of the ribosome in a purposeful way. And eventually it emerged that the ribosome was constructing ribbons of protein molecules in a way that resembled a zipper, using messenger RNA as the template. The RNA in turn was an expanded, or decoded, version of DNA in the cell nucleus. It was originally believed that RNA was just an expanded version of DNA, but chromosomes contain many instructions for different versions of RNA to emerge from a single DNA. Essentially, the ribosome then make many copies of RNA, once the particular expanded version has been selected and decoded.

You can get some idea of what cellular life is all about, by learning that every cell has hundreds of ribosome molecules strung out on a sort of net, called the reticulum. Every cell of everybody's body, or dinosaur body, or leaves on every tree, is full of a great many zippers, all busily churning out wads of duplicate proteins. And most cells are made up of proteins, doing something or other to neighbor proteins. Presumably, most diseases consist of abnormally modified proteins, and future drug therapies will require huge vats of modified proteins, calculated to dilute, modify or supplant abnormal ones. Looking back on centuries of chemistry experiments with small molecules, we can easily imagine

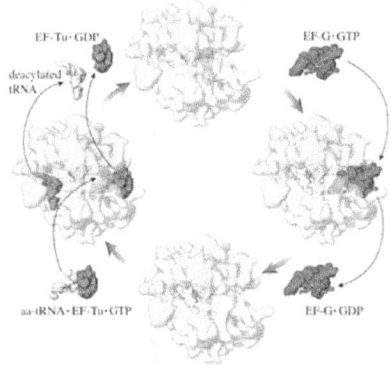

Ribosomes

that the past history of drug chemistry is only a minute happenstance in an environment which is largely made up of big proteins. Chemical boutiques redesigning and modifying new RNA proteins are easily imagined, and Joachim Frank has certainly discovered the elements of how to make such new drugs, by the ton.

http://www.philadelphia-reflections.com/blog/2662.htm

Decline and Fall of Philadelphia

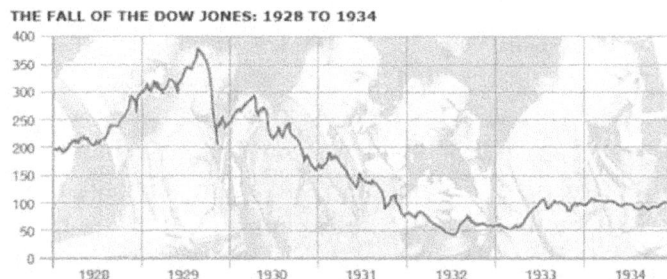

THE FALL OF THE DOW JONES: 1928 TO 1934

We talk high finance here, so perhaps a simple story from Wall Street is needed to introduce the topic to a non-Wall Street audience. Following the 1929 crash, and consequent to the Glass Steagall Act, Morgan Stanley was the only American investment bank in existence. It was the first of a new kind, but barely in existence, doing something like $300,000 worth of business in 1933. As finance adjusted to the new ground rules, Morgan Stanley grew in size, commonly referred to as the "White Shoe" investment bank. That term was an allusion to the Ivy League background of its partners, who came from colleges which affected white buckskin shoes among their more elite students. It also referred to the fact that almost all Morgan Stanley partners were pretty rich and fairly young, entirely able to live by a code of behavior which might be summarized as, "We don't find it necessary to cheat."

Morgan Stanley

Buried within that motto was the idea that Morgan Stanley was as good as its word, and tried very hard to avoid doing business with anybody who did cheat. In a business where a great deal of business was transacted too quickly for written contracts, or vetting by law firms, that meant a lot.

Buy And Sell

Morgan Stanley soon climbed to the top of a very tough heap, and stayed there for fifty years. Many of its partners were millionaires in their twenties, but so what, they were mostly pretty rich before they joined the firm. The company ran as a partnership, with the capital they leveraged coming from the personal fortunes of the partners. Under these circumstances, it is not surprising many partners retired in their forties, taking their enhanced capital with them. The Glass-Steagall Act (now being imitated by the Volcker Rule within the Dodd-Frank Law) made it illegal for a depository bank to be under the same roof with an investment bank. Much of the capital in the pre-1929 days had been supplied by the deposits in the depository bank, but Glass Steagall cut that off when it created depository insurance, on the theory that deposit insurance was a Federal gift, and its "moral hazard" should not flow through to the speculation of investment banking.

That comment was tinged with populism, with the dubious implication that those who are two generations off the farm are less likely to cheat, than those who are five generations off the farm. So the depository bank of Morgan Guaranty was split away from the investment bank of Morgan Stanley, which was the three-step process by which Morgan Stanley eventually grew so big it could no longer be sustained by leveraging the personal wealth of its partners.

Eventually, the pressure to raise money by selling stock to the public could no longer be resisted. The rich partners became even richer by selling their company's stock on the stock exchange, the company did grow enormously, and a lot of new stockholders got rich, too. Unfortunately, when you sell stock you also sell voting rights, so the sale transferred voting control of the company to the new stock purchasers. It did not take many years before the white shoe atmosphere was a thing of the past, along with the discipline that atmosphere imposed on the rest of corporate America. When the 2008 crash came along, there was enough questionable behavior on Wall Street to justify a populist President of the United States to tolerate, or even encourage, a witch hunt of Wall Street bankers for ruining the country.

Even so brilliant an economist as Paul Volcker has encouraged the idea that separating the two forms of banks was an unmitigated blessing which must be restored, while in fact it is only justified by the gift of Federal Deposit Insurance to the depository arm, not the Investment Banking Arm. It seems only a matter of time before there will be agitation to extend the insurance to the investment arm, so we will be chasing our own tail, of extending insurance to encourage risk-taking, instead of using demand deposits to do so. And thus inviting another crash.

I'm sorry, Paul, but there is a reversed way to describe it. The small investors demanded the entitlement of risk-free investing, protected by deposit insurance. And they declared this insurance was a special entitlement to which wealthy players were ineligible. When small punters go broke, it is a tragedy. When big players go broke, it serves them right for being so greedy.

 No matter. The point of the story is not the value of Glass Steagall, but rather the enormous power of Wall Street, to force a partnership to become a stockholder company, even so mighty a company as the House of Morgan. Because I have become persuaded, and hope to persuade the public, that this is the main mechanism which humbled Philadelphia, from being the mightiest industrial engine in the world, in less than twenty years. Like the perfect storm, it took three other forces to make it quite so violent, and quite so swift. They were the first World War, the 1929 stockmarket crash, and Prohibition. The central operational lever of force was exerted by: converting industrial corporations, from partnerships into stockholder corporations. That was the tool which destroyed the old Philadelphia. The other three forces simply made it happen in certain ways and at certain times.

Converting partnership or family businesses into stockholder organizations was a universal outcome of both World Wars, all over the world. The phenomenon can be looked at as one way of extracting frozen wealth to pay war debts. It is accompanied by an increase in national indebtedness, so it makes civilizations less stable. Scraps of partnership control do continue to persist in remote developing countries, and in tiny principalities like Luxembourg, but it seems only a matter of time before the public buys them out. The only major developed country to retain family control of businesses, is Germany. Apparently it was intentional, based on the inheritance laws. Tightly held

Gasoline

countries are more commonly tightly held together by force, as in Russia, Saudi Arabia, and Monaco, usually because of a monopoly grip on oil or other natural resources. But even those governments could probably be toppled, except for fear of ensuing chaos, just as did happen to many former dictatorships, and was a source of fear in Philadelphia. A case can be made for populism, if it be kept small and under control. Hardly any case at all can be made for chaos.

 For those of us who love Philadelphia and wonder what happened to it, let me point out three defining local peculiarities. Prohibition was more of a factor than we like to think, because Philadelphia's Tenderloin was the former Brewerytown, filled with Beer Gardens, refrigeration plants (Lager beer is brewed in the cold) and beer distributors. The passage of the Volstead Act suddenly transformed the largest alcohol-production center in the country into the largest alcohol-consuming area, from River to River, from Franklin Square to the Schuylkill.

Brewerytown Map It was concentrated in the Brewerytown by being illegal, and somewhat secret. Brewerytown soon turned into the Tenderloin, and the Tenderloin into Skid Row, cutting off North Philadelphia from law and order, but in time it was alarming in a different way to see speakeasies spread into other sections of the city. Much as it tried, even the Mafia couldn't control the influx of amateur criminals, when the Tenderloin essentially cut the city in half.

When the great migration from the South occurred after WW II, the immigrants turned North Philadelphia into a slum. Cutting I76 along the same center-city lines helped shrivel North Philadelphia and hustle its flight to the suburbs. Some misadventures of Philco and Ford, Baldwin and Stetson hastened the process, and may have caused some of it.

Pennsylvania Railroad

America grew into a mighty industrial nation as a result of becoming the Arsenal of Freedom in the Civil War and two World Wars. The nation needed to expand its industrial base from the essentially monopoly corridor of the Pennsylvania Railroad, and it had the money to do so. Land was cheaper elsewhere, labor was nonunion elsewhere, and air conditioning made the South bearable. Wall Street saw an enormous opportunity to buy stock from the family partners of Philadelphia industries, and sell it again to the world. These new owners had no interest in preserving lovable Philadelphia; they wanted to reap the harvest of expanding what we had, to the rest of the country, maybe even the rest of the world.

Once a spiral like this gets started, it runs by itself. The owners of the mansions on the hills, proprietors of what were big businesses by Victorian standards, sold their partnerships, their children were converted into coupon clippers, and their grandchildren into trust-fund babies. If you really have nothing much to do, why not do it in California next to the beaches? Hollywood made trust fund babies seem glamorous on the Main Line, just as Madison Avenue had once made expatriates on the left bank seem fatally attractive. Those movies and novels made somebody pretty rich, but whoever it was, doesn't live here, any more.

http://www.philadelphia-reflections.com/blog/2677.htm

All Right, Hippocrates. So What's the Basic Problem?

It took me a chapter to describe what went wrong with the Affordable Care Act. Five chapters to describe what should be done about it, in whole or in part. But the best final goal of it all, one which has the best chance of making medical care affordable, can be described in a few words. Until we decide where we want to go, we are unlikely to go there. And I simply can't believe that modification of health insurance is worthy of

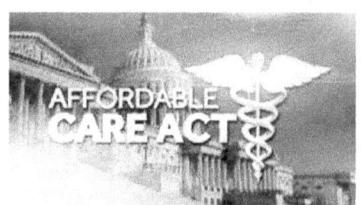

Affordable Care Act

all this uproar. Health insurance executives may be forgiven for thinking so, but it is hard to imagine the rest of the nation has such priorities. Without stopping to argue that unprovable point, I offer what I believe is a self-evident, and better, goal. One paragraph more of history is needed.

Medical turmoil in its present form seems to have begun in the Progressive Era, sometimes called the Gilded Age, which briefly preceded and probably had something to do with, the

AMA

First World War. It certainly involved President Teddy Roosevelt, who first proposed National Health Insurance, generating considerable appeal within the American Medical Association. After a brief flirtation, the Association then changed its position and has been more or less opposed ever since. At that time, the AMA turned its attention to the so-called Flexner Report of 1914, which advocated the physical and managerial relocation of medical education into the existing Universities. Out of this grew an unexpectedly vigorous medical research environment, responsible in time for the amazing transformation of medical care which characterized the 20th Century. This transformation which in turn probably generated the idea that Medical Schools were the natural center of the profession, a suggestion which greatly annoyed the AMA, triggering an unfortunate power struggle between medical school faculty and their practicing alumni. Since this battle divided those who were paid salaries from those whose income came from patient fees, parochial teaching issues were allowed to migrate into conflicts about how all doctors should be paid. From that the two groups soon split over the payment arrangements of health insurance, which also seeped out into questions of how all "health" care employees were to be paid, especially nurses, and thus who should manage them. In short, the subject material for a restructuring of medical payment wandered around for a century, getting further and further from resolution as new voices were heard, times changed, and the new arguments had little to do with the old ones. To summarize this century of argument in a few sentences leaves everyone confused about the topic, but certainly leaves no participant in a position to criticize the others. It is even possible to claim this bickering was good for the profession, because for all the scolding, medical care has undeniably flourished in the meantime. I only picked up the trail, joining the profession during the Second World War. I was a practicing physician for fifteen years before Medicare made its appearance. My viewpoint may be narrow, but I have been at work in Medicine before, during, and after most of the major changes in medical care of the last seventy years.

To come to the present concluding point, I believe the American medical system actually does have its own unique plan already for the future of health care. Never mind what the rest of the world does; they never had the resources to do what comes naturally to Americans. It goes like this: **We resolved without saying so, to pour tons of money, in amounts the Europeans cannot even imagine, into a medical system populated by the best students we could identify. This somewhat pampered priesthood has one main mission: eliminate disease, and thereby eliminate the cost of disease for everyone, rich or poor, the world over.** Some physicians are more idealistic than others, and there is some grumbling. But scarcely anyone dares to challenge the results, summarized by thirty years of increased life expectancy achieved in a single century. Arithmetic alone makes it impossible to repeat that performance.

Sounds pretty grandiose, doesn't it? As to costs, how much do we spend, today, on polio, tuberculosis, rheumatic heart disease, and thirty other diseases I once spent my time with? And how little will we soon be spending on Hepatitis C, and HIV? A lot, at first, but in ten years, probably very little. The great killers of my medical student days, like syphilis, subacute endocarditis, heart attacks and strokes, are declining fast, to probably no more than a quarter of what they used to be. People have their gall bladders and appendices removed, but they don't even go to the operating room to do it. Improved longevity is taken for granted. Doesn't anyone want to live an extra thirty years? Doesn't everyone want his cataracts and knees replaced? The list goes on so long it is ineffective to recite it. We got our orders, and we delivered. No other nation on earth could even dream of such a project, and yet someone still occasionally challenges me with statistics about infant mortality in Luxembourg. Our inpatient psychiatry is a disgrace, yes I will give you that. But wipe out disease, that's the way to reduce health care costs for everyone. We're going to do it, and nobody else has a prayer of a chance. It is remarkable that costs keep rising while disease keeps disappearing, but even that trend must come to an end. Inevitably, there will be a reckoning of details.

It's probably fair to ask who told us to do such a thing. Everybody did, and nobody did. As much as anybody, my contemporary at the NIH, Jim Shannon exemplified this dream of the conquest of disease, and was in a position to do something about it. Maybe it was Vannevar Bush, who was the same sort of scientific evangelist. But somehow that search doesn't feel like the right one. What feels right is that the generation of Americans who conquered the armies of the world, just pushed us onward to conquer a little thing like disease. American exceptionalism did it, and right or wrong is going to get it done. It's true that I worry we

NIH, Jim Shannon

will keep people on thirty year vacations, which our grandchildren will

Vannevar Bush

take at the beginning of life instead of the end of it. It begins to sound as though Reverend Malthus may have been right about feeding all these people, and maybe there will be problems with employment. But that isn't our mission. We feel the nation wanted very badly for us to do what we did, and they are just going to have to whip up a generation of environmentalists, or sociologists, or banjo players – if there are to be new directives. Passerby, go tell the Spartans: We lie here, forever obedient to their laws.

Since I am about to launch, in closing, a proposal for revising the goals of American health care, it seems appropriate to begin it by recalling a remark of one of my medical school teachers, delivered at the close of the Second World War. "The goals for medical research," said this pathologist, "are relatively small. When we've found a cure for cancer and arteriosclerosis, we're about done." Since the current generation of students would regard anything known before 1945 as not worth knowing, and the treatment of cancer has not advanced much since the time of this prophecy, we had best be modest about what we already know. It is widely stated that fifty percent of drugs currently in use, were totally unknown only seven years ago. That may well be true, and may continue to be true for centuries to come. The limits of knowledge for medical students were once defined in a study by Howard Becker called *Boys in White* and go as follows: First year medical students are determined to learn it all. By sophomore year they have decided you can't possibly learn it all, so you only try to learn what is important. By Junior year even that seems impossible to learn, so you only try to learn what is going to be on the tests. Essentially what this says is that the faculty finally gets control of things by Junior year, and their selectivity defines the horizons of what students pay any attention to.

This is a strangely limited selection of topics, which is finally set straight by the training directors of postgraduate Residency programs. Having played each of these roles in my time, I feel the residency directors have it about right, but only for inpatient care. Outpatient care is now the source of nearly half of hospital revenue, and the proportion is rapidly growing. The inpatient faculty reasserts control by writing the Board Examinations, and the final mixture is defined as the present state of medical knowledge, but it remains strangely neglectful of the outpatient half of medical care (notice, I did not say health care, which has become a rapidly growing world as non physicians assert control over funding sources).

But even an assessment based on all these biases may still not be a good measure of where Society stands in its search for scientific progress. For one thing, we haven't been serious about science for very long. The first course in science, of any sort in any American university, was only offered at the time of the Civil War. Although I had already decided to enter the Medical Profession by the Second World War (eighty years later), I nevertheless chose a college major more suitable for a gentleman. English literature, now that was the thing. In a a few elite colleges, it still is. A bachelor in engineering is a degree for people who invent things; a bachelor in science was for those who would discover things. But a bachelor in the Arts, was a degree for someone who planned to run things. Until that witticism loses its bite, we haven't really become serious about how much we can depend on the average patient knowing what he needs to know, to assume cost-effective control of his health. Young women and mothers chatter about pediatric topics quite a lot, but for the rest of the population the state of medical information remains what the physician priesthood understands and has the time to communicate.

In 1945, the limits of medical knowledge were thus only two: how to cure cancer, and what to do about atherosclerosis. Today, we finally discover that sleep has a lot to do with the circulation of spinal fluid through the brain, which sounds about as advanced as Harvey's discovery of the circulation of blood in 1642. This year it became possible to see that protein synthesis is like a zipper in thousands of ribosome molecules inside zillions of cells inside you, me, Eucalyptus leaves, and dinosaur bones. Since cellular chemistry is pretty much protein chemistry, the potential for drug synthesis, to say nothing of understanding cell activities, is immense. I have had a reasonable acquaintance with a couple dozen Nobel Prize winners, and mostly I don't know what they are talking about. The point is this: right now, it is practically impossible to know how much more there is to know, and therefore what discoveries are possible in the next twenty-five to fifty years. My pathology professor was obviously pitifully ignorant in 1945 about what lay ahead, and we haven't even cured cancer yet. How long it will take for a lot of billionaires to be created after they discovered a cure for something, isn't known and isn't knowable. But God bless them all, because the money they will save us in the cost of medical care, simply staggers the mind. Who will care about the cost of health insurance, when every disease the present generation of medical students will learn about, has disappeared? On the other hand, perhaps the scientific opportunities which are uncovered will trivialize the new pharmaceuticals of only seven years ago, which are half of the drugs presently in use. As long as the music keeps playing, we will have to keep dancing, and hope for the best.

http://www.philadelphia-reflections.com/blog/2669.htm

Cost Shifting: Indigent Care Out, Outpatient Revenue, In

The CEO of Safeway Stores recently offered his company's preventive approaches as an example of what the nation can do to reduce health costs. He's undoubtedly sincere, but quite wrong; Safeway just shifted costs to Medicare. This is only one of several ways, major ways, cost-shifting is misleading us. Let's explain.

Safeway Store

Average life expectancy is increasing at more than two years per decade, but of course people eventually die. Since health care costs are heaviest in the last year or two of life, extending life will soon push nearly all those heavy terminal costs from employer based insurance – into Medicare. To die at age 64 costs Blue Cross a lot; but to die at 65 gets Medicare to pay for it. Either way, the cost is exactly the same, it doesn't save Society as a whole any money at all. Let's put it another way: dying at age 64 costs the employer and the employees; but dying at 65 costs the taxpayers. This means Medicare costs will surely rise, but in this case it's a reason to rejoice.

Increasing longevity is constantly pushing more costs from employers to Medicare, and not just in Safeway; the prospect is that soon substantially all major sickness costs will shift into Medicare. (To explain the failure of most employer insurance premiums to fall comparably in response to this shift, one must look elsewhere). But just a minute. Medicare is 50% subsidized by the government, and the employer writes off half of the cost as a business expense. That ought to mean it doesn't make much difference to anyone involved, except for one thing. Some employers have two employees and some have two hundred thousand employees. The amount of tax write-off is multiplied by the number of employees, so some employers can only write off a little, while an occasional employer might even make a profit on using health insurance for calisthenics. Economists agree that fringe benefits eventually and proportionately come out of the pay packet, so ultimately the employed patient benefits from the reduced bill, his employer pays less, and the Medicare costs the taxpayers more.

Medicare

But instead of going down that trail, let's look at a second form of cost-shifting. Government payers and a few other monopolists are able to pay hospitals less than actual costs, and get away with it. The worst offenders are state governors administering Medicaid, where the underpayment is roughly 30%, in spite of federal reimbursement to the states for most of it, at full price. The resulting profit is used for various state purposes, mainly nursing home reimbursement. For the most part, such diverted funds are used for purposes not easily eliminated, so it is unlikely there will be much cost reduction for government if the scam is acknowledged and merely shifted to a different line in the ledger. To avoid bankruptcy, hospitals raise the rates for other health insurance plans – and the uninsured. Employers are paying for most of it, so they stand to gain from reform, only to face higher state taxes as matters readjust. We have yet to learn where these costs will shift if the federal government takes over the costs of the uninsured; the current Obamacare plan is to shift 15 million uninsured persons to Medicaid. To a major degree, the federal government and its taxpayers are already paying for a lot of this uninsured cost, through the Medicaid shift. So its present dilemma is whether to continue to pay for it twice.

There's still a third cost-shift. In 1983, Medicare stopped reimbursing hospitals fee-for-service (itemized inpatient bills are still prepared but are meaningless fictions) and for thirty years has paid by the diagnosis, not the service, for inpatients. Consequently, per beneficiary inpatient costs have only risen 18% in five years, while outpatient costs have risen 47%. Costs are not the same as prices, which are even worse distorted. To a large extent, changes in costs are really changes in accounting practices, driving changes in actual practices. Skilled nursing and home care costs are rising even faster. When you hear fee-for-service payments attacked, it is this apparent overpayment of outpatient costs which is the source of complaint. But to pay out-patient medical costs in any way other than fee-for-service would imply an almost unimaginable restructuring of the medical system, without any proof it would save money. It will be very interesting to learn what contorted proposal is about to emerge.

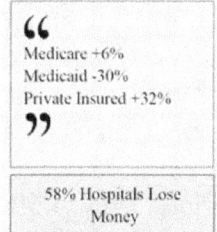

"
Medicare +6%
Medicaid -30%
Private Insured +32%
"

58% Hospitals Lose
Money

Not only do these shifts provoke inpatient nursing shortages, they start a war for patients between hospitals and office-based physicians. Hospitals are winning this war for business, but are losing money doing so. If the public ever demands a stop to loss-leaders, net insurance premiums will probably rise. The difference between a hospital which makes money and one which loses money is based on whether there is enough extra out-patient revenue to compensate for the hidden tax which the state effectively imposes on hospitals in order to pay for nursing homes. The obscurity of the present payment system is quite expensive, and the present beneficiaries of it are the Medicaid nursing homes. Obamacare essentially provides health insurance to 15 million uninsured by the process of placing them on Medicaid, so the consequences are going to be an interesting juggling act to watch.

"
5-Year Change:
Inpatient +18%
Outpatient +47%
"

5-Year Hospital
Costs

Just notice, for example, that neither Medicare nor private health insurance pays below costs, if you look at total national balances. Private insurers are paying hospitals 32% more than actual inpatient costs, while Medicare is paying 6% more than national cost. And yet 58% of hospitals are losing money. The magic in this formula lies in the losses incurred by state Medicaid but shifted to other payers. It could fairly be said we are just looking at a maldistribution of the uninsured, as a cost, and a maldistribution of non-inpatient revenues, as a profit, among the nation's hospitals. To what extent such maldistribution reflects uneven patient quality, as the loser hospitals claim, or provider inefficiency, as the winner hospitals would say, – merely starts a distraction of attention which could last twenty years while we examine it.

And disruptions enough to take decades to fix.

http://www.philadelphia-reflections.com/blog/1696.htm

Indemnity and Payment by Diagnosis: Fair Prices For Healthcare

In America, the closest thing to an oriental bazaar is the auto showroom, where a salesman will spend an hour evading the price question, knowing some customers will eventually buy a car rather than spend unlimited time shopping. Lack of price transparency favors the merchant, so prices are higher. It probably does follow that healthcare prices would be lower if prices were more widely advertised and therefore, more standard.

But healthcare also varies in quality and effectiveness, so prices need to be flexible enough to compensate. Even eminent practitioners therefore squirm at the idea of price transparency. Flexible pricing is in fact a useful thing, without it prices do rise, but not as much as supposed, and not without some justification. The practitioner is tangled in a web of comparisons, with his colleagues, with clinics and institutional salaries, with memories of other prices for nearly the same thing, with all the other alternatives available to a customer who can walk around and shop. Under the circumstances, the patients generally want to have a fond relationship with a doctor they can trust to know what the market is saying, and trust him to make the best guess about what his own services are worth. Therefore, a physician is a fiduciary, expected to put the patient's interest ahead of his own. Insurance is not a fiduciary: Our modern third-party system systematically replaces trust with: standard prices, blind faith in low prices as always better than higher ones, and determination that medical quality had better always be top-notch, or else we will sue.

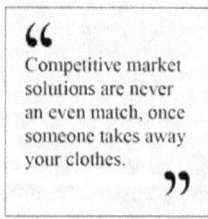

> Competitive market solutions are never an even match, once someone takes away your clothes.

Our system of third-party payment has firmly fixed its goal on a single price for the same service, no matter what its quality may be. By its very nature, a remote third-party payer cannot judge which person wasted the doctor's time, which doctor took extra care, which offices are shabby and which are unnecessarily plush. A surgeon leaves his showroom office empty most of the time he is in the operating room, while a dermatologist barely moves his feet for eight hours in the office; both of them are paid uniform rates. Any effort to modify the price in response to variables, is only listened to, if the outcome is to lower the price. The industry term for this process is "service benefits". A physical exam is a physical exam, a history is a history, a gastrostomy is a gastrostomy. Oh, yeah? If you believe that, said the Duke of Wellington, you will believe anything.

The best way to handle the situation is to pay, in part, by indemnity. In effect, indemnity makes the promise to pay $800 for a gastrostomy. If the surgeon thinks he is worth more than that, it must be agreed to by the patient in advance, and paid out-of-pocket. Not paid in advance, agreed to in advance, with the implicit understanding it can be reduced by sincere dispute, after the fact, and without recourse before the fact. Back at the beginning of the system, this feature was bargained away. I cannot resist telling the story of my father-in-law's advice to me, doctor to doctor, at the time of my wedding. "Never let your wife keep your books," said he. "To you, the patient is a poor old devil down on his luck. To your wife, he just represents a steak dinner, if she can collect the bill." Our third-party payment system has succeeded in projecting the image of protecting the patient against voracious "providers of care", just the reverse of their natural postures, and something my father in law never

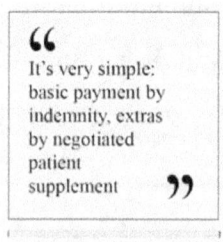

> It's very simple: basic payment by indemnity, extras by negotiated patient supplement

dreamed of. It's very simple: basic payment by indemnity, extras by negotiated patient supplement. Since consumer representatives are so intransigent about "give-backs", it might as well include a COLA on the basic, and otherwise put inflation into the patient supplement.

At this point, we should probably pause and notice that the imperfect DRG system for inpatients, has nevertheless proved to be an extremely effective rationing tool. It quite effectively put an end to relying on the bed patient to be unable to walk away. In a little research project of mine, the eighteenth century patients were in the hospital bed for exactly the same reason they are today: they couldn't walk, or couldn't be allowed to walk. Competitive market solutions are never an even match, once someone takes away your clothes. If the DRG system could be improved by substituting a better coding system (SNODO recommended), it would answer every objection except one. That objection is the relentless instinct of Society organized as institutions to squeeze payments and quality, once the helpless patient is out of sight of visitors.

At present, DRG is mainly forcing patients out who were once enticed into the hospital by the previous payment system. Once that backlog is exhausted, the DRG pressure will start to hurt, since all rationing systems lead to shortages. Like the Volstead Act, this government mandate was successful in its original purpose, but the unintended consequences were worse. When DRG starts to hurt, a new coding system had better be ready. Because the resultant growth of hospital outpatient services has been so extreme, it will cause a bigger bubble to burst unless attention is given to service benefits inflating the cost of outpatient care. To repeat, the cure for medical cost inflation is not to apply rationing, it is to improve the payment methodology so that rationing is unnecessary. The current repetitious chorus denouncing fee for service, is just a cry of desperation from people too unimaginative to devise any substitute more sophisticated than salaried rationing. The problem here is not fee for service, it is service benefits. And the problem lies, not with the provider, but with the carefree beneficiary – carefree because he is insured. And furthermore the solution is not salaried practitioners bossed by salaried politicians, it is a hybrid of indemnity with basic pricing. Under Health Savings Accounts, we bring the public into power over its own affairs. The remaining problem is to let the individual control his own monster, by making waste and luxury his affair, not an affair of the public at large. A good beginning would be to forbid the use of collection agencies, forcing the institution to confront its irate customers.

http://www.philadelphia-reflections.com/blog/2655.htm

American Exceptionalism Has Something To Do With Compromise

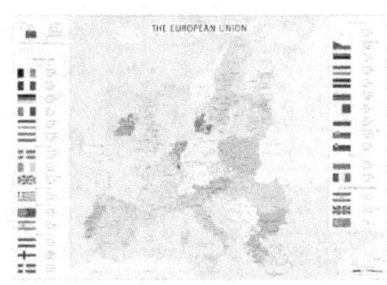

European Union Map

Let no one suppose I imagine myself an expert in international law. But as a member of a family with newspaper connections, I more readily recognize when someone is conducting a campaign, using a set of plausible arguments in place of the real ones. So, my suspicions are repeatedly reinforced by regular repetitions of the same arguments in different ways, to the effect that America should be more respectful of what is called International Law. Curiously, the same people are of a mindset to oppose European Union, when you would suppose that one argument leads to the other. It is almost a pose that, having won the war as legitimate sovereigns, they are already quashing would-be competitors.

Rhine River

Nationalism had its formal beginnings in the Treaty of Westphalia, about 1648. At that time, there were about a hundred little countries along the banks of the Rhine River, starting in Switzerland which was broken into four cantons, and south of the Swiss stretching the length of Italy, ending up in the far tip of Sicily. Many of these nations were no bigger than a golf course, and were often leftovers from the robber barons who extorted bribes from passing boats in return for not attacking them. That is, they were protection rackets, which survived as rackets in the far tip of Sicily until 1880 or so, until Garibaldi emancipated them from their evil ways, and unified Italy.

In 1648 the Pope was in nominal charge of everything, and all the rest of the Rhineland behaved the way we now think of the Mafia as behaving, in secret societies. Martin Luther's Protestant reformation had broken the Holy Roman Empire into warring camps, shifting alliances as local politics required. It took a long time to get everyone into an agreement, but the outcome was the Treaty of Westphalia, which essentially made everyone agree to respect the national

Treaty of Westphalia

boundaries of the others, and the religion of the inhabitants of each country would adopt the religion of the local king. There had been nations before there was nationalism, but the Westphalian version operated with national boundaries as the defined beginning, rather than tribes, languages or religions. That sort of agreement displeased the Pope, of course, but it had the utility of lessening the endless warfare and pillage, each one of each other. Offhand, you might not have thought of boundaries as superior to ethnic inhabitants as an organizing principle, but somehow it worked better than the alternatives. Nationalism became the ruling premise throughout the world. If you win, your winnings are limited to the established boundaries. The treaty of Westphalia served essentially as constitution for a majority of western civilizations, and it was pretty short and sweet, essentially downgrading religion as an organizing principle and replacing it with defensible boundaries, seemingly a degrading change.

City Tavern

Eventually, thirteen "sovereign nations" in the Western Hemisphere got together and wrote our new Constitution, which had an additional novelty of being written down and describing how the new United States would be organized. Religion was banished from governance, of course, so the way was open to our own nationalism. Among other features was a bicameral legislature. Pennsylvania in 1787 had just had a lot of trouble with a unicameral legislature, but the main impetus opposing that format was found in the small states. John Dickinson of Dover Delaware drew a startled James Madison of Virginia aside, and told him the small states didn't like being bossed by the big ones (Virginia was the largest, at that time), and they particularly disliked the idea that it would be written down as a permanent arrangement. In the view of the big states, power would naturally go to the biggest and richest, and that infuriated the small states even more. To them, it meant the small states were expected to pay permanent deference to the ideas of their bigger neighbors, and for example no one from a small state could ever expect to be elected President. Dickinson drew Madison aside and asked, "Do you want to have a Union, or don't you?" Dickinson was probably thinking in terms of equal representation for each state, no matter its size, while Madison was thinking of proportional representation like the House of Representatives. Rumor has it that Benjamin Franklin gathered folks into the City Tavern and worked out the present compromise. Which is, a bicameral legislature, one body with two and only two Senators per state, the second body with additional representatives for more population, and the agreement that no law would be passed without the agreement of both houses of Congress. Pretty simple, but it has gradually dawned on most people that the United State has held together (Civil War excepted) for two hundred years by debate and compromise, but meanwhile no other union has survived by any means except military force. Underneath that rule must be an assumption: for every quarrel, somewhere there exists a workable compromise. Even Ben Franklin was a little hesitant about that idea.

League of Nations, United Nations

The League of Nations, United Nations, and all of the other national groupings, so far including even the European Union, have unicameral legislatures which follow the traditions of the Treaty of Westphalia. Equal representation for all, and therefore majority rule is expected to leave major groups nursing a grudge. In a bicameral state with different rules for election, the ruling instruction is "Don't you come out of that room until you agree on some compromise which will endure." A bicameral legislature is expected to produce flawed legislation; a unicameral body is expected to produce a victory. Therefore, a unicameral is expected to produce a vanquished foe; a bicameral needs cooperation to justify flawed legislation and keep it workable. As things work out, there is no perfect law, only laws which are more or less imperfect.

"On the whole, sir, I cannot help expressing a wish that every member of the convention who may still have objections to it, would, with me, on this occasion, doubt a little of his own infallibility, and, to make manifest our unanimity, put his name to this instrument."

http://www.philadelphia-reflections.com/blog/2649.htm

Ads Age

Blogs pop
Non stop
Screens surge
Stars urge
Be quick
Just click
Day long
Sell song

    Urge spend
    No end
    Hope greed
    Trumps need
    Mind pleas
    Cease sprees
    What's heard
    Buy word

Air Heads

Tech kid
Gets rid
Old gear
Each year
Must flings
Hot things
Gross size
Net buys

    Too soon
    Next boon
    Makes now
    No how
    Pen pals
    Guys gals
    Loves hates
    Cell mates

Barn Storm

Pols win
Stay in
Work charm
Bet farm
Sow oats
Reap votes
Hands pump
Stomp stump

    Fat cows
    Push plows
    Love pace
    Horse race
    Burst stall
    Win all
    Whole hog
    Top dog

Biz Buzz

Men meet
Chat greet
Eyes lock
Fists knock
Then food
Sets mood
Talk shop
Non stop

    These meals
    Do deals
    Words hum
    Near numb
    Drone on
    Wax strong
    Wins see
    King bee

Brass Ring

Spring rite
Dreams bright
Teams race
First place
Sure shot
Wins pot
Ends drought
Pans out

All aim
Stake claim
Make rounds
Grab crowns
Hopes new
Comes through
Not old
Fools gold

Bum Wraps

Ads tout
Those stout
Lose flaps
Boast abs
Hopes high
Must try
Thin yen
Goal ten

Work buns
Brief runs
Yet pounds
Stay rounds
Friends chaff
Smug laugh
Slow pokes
Butt jokes

Check Mate

Who'll be
For me
Best wife
All Life
Good friends
Nice blends
Starts fun
Move on

But when
Lags yen
Bored game
Slow same
Must split
That's it
Bad patch
Ends match

Choice Cuts

Long run
Less fun
Some wait
Trust fate
They find
Slow grind
Take grief
Don't beef

Those keen
Choose lean
Don't stew
Quick do
Dash fleet
Win meat
Right breaks
Prime steaks

Chop Shop

Set sail
For sale
Where crowd
Mills loud
Long lines
Test spines
Shout stores
"Spend more"

Vast sea
Park free
All barge
To charge
Bump buy
That's why
They call
It maul

Churn Pike

Cars crawl
Swerve stall
Lines stop
Then pop
Curse cry
Fists fly
Hearts race
Slow pace

Blue sights
Red lights
All blame
Rush game
Near crash
Teeth gnash
Jaws block
Grit Lock

Crass Act

Year book
Gives look
Shows cast
Of past
Splash notes
Faux quotes
Word games
Slang names

Kind phrase
Brings praise
Smart style
Sprouts smile
Friends dear
Hearts cheer
Class Clowns
Brass sounds

Dead Lines

When gone
Sad Song
Brief Note
Short Quote
Life Acts
Cold Facts
That's It
Says Wit

Old Age
Reads Page
As Friends
Meet Ends
Shed Tear
Toast Bier
Such Sights
Last Writes

Dis Cuss

Teens shout
Scream Flout
Foul words
In herds
From mild
To wild
No pride
Free ride

    Low class
    Like brass
    Pray soon
    Change tune
    Shocks pale
    Turn stale
    They scoff
    Swear off

Fit Fits

My size
No prize
Waist grows
Past clothes
Suck in
Friends grin
If squeeze
All tease

    Next phase
    Change weights
    Pride learns
    Stem sterns
    End gape
    Shift shape
    Must charge
    Buy large

Fore Casts

Golf Green
Fun Scene
Hit ball
Shout call
Bad guess
Scores mess
Right aim
Ace game

    Some say
    This play
    Mines Dow
    Charts how
    Right pitch
    Ducks ditch
    Good lies
    Trap prize

Frame Ups

When bowl
Feel whole
Throw ball
Give all
Fast lanes
Ease pains
Spares strikes
Spike pshchs

    Watch pros
    Smooth throws
    Hooks curves
    Soothe nerves
    Times good
    Knock wood
    Top score
    Bowled 'Ore

Friend-ship

First grade
Mate made
Teen time
Pals bind
School too
Guys glue
Grad hits
Groups split

Launch forth
South north
Past crew
Rings true
Last dock
Take stock
When old
Bonds hold

Gilt Trip

Gem sale
Rings wail
Gals much
Love touch
Eyes squint
Starts glint
Their prayer
To wear

Buy word
Is heard
First oohs
Then choose
She's bold
Digs gold
From wine
To mine

Got Cha

Dance craze
Wins praise
Watch pros
Head toes
Lads lass
Show class
Feet fly
Trip try

Step one
Have fun
Some win
Shoe in
Fear not
Last spot
Joys burst
Feat first

Grad Rags

' Lums Back
Sing yack
First pick
Old Clique
Swap tales
New ails
Turn page
On age

Some shun
Such fun
See bores
Old sores
But most
Make toast
Past said
Well bred

Enforcing the Constitution: Civil Monetary Penalties (CMP)

The 1787 Constitution created three branches of government along with their defined powers, but described no remedy for a branch overstepping its boundaries. Gradually, a system evolved for declaring some laws unconstitutional, one by one, clarifying individual issues along the way. By contrast, the founding fathers viewed the President as an agent of Congress, expecting Congress to devise controls if needed. George Washington had an intense distaste for monarchs, and eight years as Commander in Chief had exposed no taste for conflict with the Continental Congress. Unfortunately, this has proven to be unusual for Presidents, especially as popular sovereignty appears to expand the Presidential mandate. Moreover, Washington himself developed more friction with Congress during his two terms as President.

Founding Fathers

In retrospect, the main factor behind Presidential restlessness is the experience of misinterpreting the meaning of a broader electoral mandate, which can more properly be traced to hasty repair of the defects of the 1800 election process. Experience has shown that while ignoring rules invites anarchy, impeachment of a President usually seems too drastic a remedy for unwelcome innovation, while impeaching the whole Legislative Branch for failure to supervise in a general way, is incomprehensible. The President needs some sort of supervision. While the original intent was to have Congress do the supervising, the Supreme Court is now probably better suited for judging the issue of unconstitutional behavior, except for the awkwardness that the President appoints the Supreme Court. These are the simple ingredients of a solution, preferably unwritten and revolving around conferring special "standing" in special circumstances.

Chief Justice, John Marshall

At present, grievances tend to accumulate until someone acquires "standing" by being injured. At present it is generally true a grievance scarcely matters if no one is injured, but the exception is the lack of redress for injury to the Constitution, whereby everyone may be injured. Furthermore, actual experience with creeping boundary encroachment has mostly proved to be nuanced, rather than confrontational, gradual rather than abrupt. The descriptive example is that of a frog in a gradually heated pan of water, whereby the frog is cooked faster than he realizes he is in danger. Otherwise, the courts have evolved an unspecified balance which has proved remarkably serviceable.

It took thirty years for John Marshall to formulate the general approach needed. In *Marbury v. Madison*, his first action after becoming Chief Justice, John Marshall suggested a writ of *Mandamus* (i.e. "We command...") from the Court might well be the first step in what he coyly described as only a hypothetical situation. Only lawyers were expected to recognize fully that If the President ignored the writ, then the grounds for impeachment might escalate, with the President forced into the role of flouting a decision of the Court. Regardless of how it stood on the original issue, the public would likely support a Court in performing its duty to make difficult decisions.

One way or another, the national issue would become one of whether the nation wished to continue with its Constitution; Marshall had only outlined the steps the process would probably take. At several points along the way, the Chief Justice would have a chance to back off. But Marshall's lifelong hatred of his cousin Thomas Jefferson was so well known there was little doubt he was serious. Knowing of his cousin's hatred for him, President Jefferson let the matter drop; subsequent Presidents followed his example. Generations of lawyers have studied this case and pondered its implications. The solution to the problem of extending it from unconstitutional laws to unconstitutional behavior, probably already exists in many minds.

http://www.philadelphia-reflections.com/blog/2659.htm

Philadelphia's Real Estate Gridlock

It was spoken hurriedly, and I don't remember who said it. But the gist was that Philadelphia had been the richest city in the world in 1900. In the World, mind you. I can scarcely believe that, but the way it stuck with me shows it had some substance. Rather than comparing Philadelphia with London, New York City, or Paris, I must now compare that exuberance with the dirty, dejected, defeated old wreck of a Philadelphia I first encountered in 1948. Baltimore, Newark and a dozen old American cities sort of crumbled into dust after 1929, but Philadelphia briefly seemed to be picking up in 1948. Richardson Dilworth was getting ready to run for Mayor, and the town's newspapers even enjoyed the idea of a Philadelphia revival. But then the Pennsylvania Railroad collapsed, and after that we just struggled along, neither dying nor recovering. Some of both, perhaps, but more dying than recovering, and making it credible to believe that Philadelphia just never did recover from the 1929 crash. Just think of that; from top to bottom in thirty years. There just had to be some better explanation than bad management of one railroad.

Until recently, I had accepted the general wisdom that stock market crashes are followed by depressions. Perhaps I am a little slow, but there never seemed to be any question of that analysis, since all major crashes really were followed by recessions, going back to 1792 when Philadelphia had the first American version, and the first financier villain, someone named William Duer. Or maybe it was Robert Morris. Or maybe it was Thomas Mifflin, but in any event it was someone very rich who did something very reprehensible which toppled the stock market and plunged the rest of us poor victims into protracted suffering. In other scenes of carnage, it had been John Bull, or William Whitney, or Nicholas Biddle. Or J.P. Morgan, that monster. In the 2007 crash it wasn't so much one villain as one company, Goldman Sachs, or maybe Lehman Brothers. Since the recent crash was so recent, and news coverage so rapid, it might be easier to trace out who the villain was. But there was no one real villain, and even if we found one, it was hard to see why a few days of choked markets would still be causing unemployment seven years later. No one seemed to know, or at least no one wanted to tell me, why stock market crashes cause depressions. They are certainly followed by depressions.

And then suddenly I realized, or maybe someone just broke the news to me, that I had it all backward. Market crashes don't cause depressions, depressions cause market crashes. First, the markets get overheated, everyone gets uneasy, but everyone is making the most money in his life. Suddenly, someone sells out, like shouting "fire" in a crowded theater, and everyone tries to get out the door at the same time. The catastrophe makes everyone see that stocks or real estate, bonds or tulip bulbs, had become ridiculously overpriced, so nobody will buy them at any price. But let's not get down into the weeds of market technicality; prices got disconnected from real values. We overproduced something, or even everything, and things wouldn't improve until somebody needed something he had stopped needing, several years earlier. Maybe there were villains, there are always plenty of villains. But we wanted somebody to blame, because otherwise everybody has to take some blame. We needed, in short, a scapegoat.

So let's ask the question again: what caused the great depression of the thirties? And the best answer to come back was, the First World War. Philadelphia was the arsenal of democracy, the maker of ships and gunpowder and uniforms. The great transatlantic ocean port, the embarkation point. If we weren't sending troops we were sending tanks and airplanes. The duPonts were sending gunpowder to France, a way of paying back Beaumarchais for sending gunpowder from France to the Battle of Trenton. After their wars were over, one Frenchman went back to making wristwatches and writing plays, and the other munitions maker swore off gunpowder and concentrated on nylon stockings. That's far too simple. Philadelphia had expanded and expanded to exploit its wartime advantages. When the war was over the boom was over, but the roaring Twenties roared. They built mansions, clear out to Paoli and beyond. Movies were written about our heroes, who left their jewelry in the vaults of the Girard Bank after the opera while they went back to the horse country at four in the morning. It seems a virtual certainty that no one who acted like that, knew what every MBA from Temple now knows: real estate is just about the only link for ordinary people between interest rates and consumption. All assets contribute somewhat to the "Wealth Effect", but real estate is usually the only channel the average person can find, as a way to translate major assets into consumer goods. And since a stock market crash will lower interest rates, the ensuing low cost of mortgages stimulates a real estate boom. Office buildings in the city, mansions in the horse country. But then the city loses its postwar boom, and soon loses a million or more population. Result: empty office buildings, empty mansions. Along Spruce and Pine Streets, people moved out of the grand houses and into the servants' houses in the back alleys. Easier to heat.

A friend of mine, whose occupation is locating real estate for businesses, tells me the startling news that land around Philadelphia is too expensive for factories. It seemed hardly credible that real estate could seem so hard to sell, with "For Sale" signs lining the curbs, and yet seem too overpriced for a company to locate here. Suburban Philadelphia house prices were depressed during the Depression so that a seven bedroom Main Line house couldn't find a buyer, but the land was still too expensive for a factory; and anyway the zoning wouldn't permit a business. Our suburban and exurban land got chopped up into residential real estate, streets were built, sewer lines were extended for miles, trees and ornamentals were planted. Schools and shopping centers were built, maybe some museums and hospitals. But none of that was attractive for a business, and you can't attract an executive to residential real estate without a place to go to work. The features attractive to his wife, were not enough to attract him and his business. He wants cheap open land to build factories and vast parking spaces for employees. He doesn't want to get fifty miles away from the port that made

Philadelphia prosperous. And he particularly doesn't want to spend his time going to protest meetings about smoke and pollution, or go to court to defend his ownership of what someone else polluted, a century earlier. He particularly doesn't want to go to Planned Parenthood meetings with his wife, in order to be hassled about carbon fuels or greenhouse gases in China. Sorry, he's going to build his new plant in North Carolina. And the residential real estate couldn't be made cheap enough for that purpose without tearing down the house, and the schools, and maybe the shopping center. Once the land becomes dedicated, you have to choose: either a nice suburb, or a place favorable for a business.

A former President of a Federal Reserve Bank located a thousand miles from Philadelphia was recently here for a conference, and at loose ends for someone to chat with. To my astonishment, he exploded with rage when he contemplated Mr. Obama's refusal to sign permission to build a pipeline from Canada to the Gulf of Mexico. To him, it was obvious that the main thing holding back the American economy was a refusal of American businesses to invest in new plants and equipment. The banks were stuffed with money, but business refused to borrow it. The Federal Reserve was powerless to stimulate an economy that didn't want to expand, forever pointing to uncertainties of expanding in the face of a regulatory authority which seemed determined to thwart them, to browbeat and humiliate them in front of TV. It isn't personal, it is serious; because the quarrel is ultimately about important economics. A dollar in 1913 when the Federal Reserve was created, is now worth a penny, and there is every indication of administration eagerness to see the present dollar only worth a penny, far sooner than a century from now. The man speaking was obviously sincere and deeply upset, and what seemed to bother him most was the perception that "the environmentalists" are equally sincere, and thus equally unready to give an inch. The economist regarded the argument of the environmentalists as irrelevant to what was really important, just as surely as the environmentalists were heedless of any legitimacy in the arguments for savaging wildlife. Neither side saw this in terms of city versus suburbs, or agriculture versus commuters. Neither seemed to acknowledge that a city based on concentric rings had to break the ring pattern in order to maintain harmonious balance between living well and making a living. That is, until the two sides recognize they are talking about the same problem on some level, it will be a dialogue of the deaf, offering no possible resolution except war to the death. It's become a religious conflict, with both sides heedless of things vital to the other side.

They say the main function of real estate brokers is to maintain high prices for property values. But in the long run, if a region isn't prosperous, its residential property will lose value, not gain it.

http://www.philadelphia-reflections.com/blog/2658.htm

Too Much Money

Globalization may well have created a thousand billionaires, but its benefits to poor people were greater. As a guess, five hundred million desperately poor people were lifted out of poverty, and eventually it may be several billion. For a certainty, we will soon need a new definition of poverty, which only a few years ago was to subsist on less than a dollar a day. Rich or poor, these lucky people were not the objects of charity, but the visible beneficiaries of enormous wealth creation, surely the greatest gold rush in human history.

The Gold Rush

If they buy guns and bombs (or narcotics) with their new money, we may not be so happy about its unintended consequences. So far, however, the major unintended consequences have been benign upheavals, like the rapid spread of the computer and internet revolutions, the extension of life expectancy and literacy. These reasonably benign side-revolutions have bounced back as accelerators of the boom. The unit cost of transactions has plummeted; nerdy mathematicians have advanced into the murky mist of derivatives. No one doubted self-seeking bosses would abuse the extraordinary insights of their intellectual superiors, and they did, indeed. It's probably true that wise observers predicted this would all end in tears. And it did.

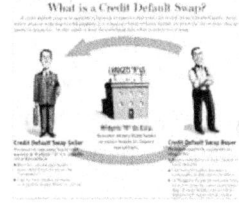
Credit Default Swaps

We are now in the midst of the usual witch-hunt for perpetrators, because we have a national election every four years. Both political parties are planning to spend a billion dollars accusing each other, so the accusations will surely get louder before they calm down. But in the spirit of directing the anger toward more productive targets, it should be remembered that harm to the public usually originates as incompetence, rather than greed. About five years before the crash, for example, I found myself adrift in a convention of bank officers. Within fifteen minutes, I satisfied myself that not one vice-president in the room could offer a coherent definition of a derivative. The general public still cannot define it, but everybody thinks he can recognize greed: it's someone with more money than you have. A few weeks before the initial crash in August, 2007, I was made aware that things called Credit Default Swaps were in circulation in the amount of twenty-five trillion dollars. It was impossible for me to find anyone or any search engine which could tell me what these confounded CDS things were, even though their quantity exceeded what I understood to be the national debt of the United States. And their quantity was doubling every few months. A few months

Federal Reserve

later, indeed, it was made clear that the national debt was far larger than anyone thought. There's a great temptation in a situation like this to demand that Congress pass a law to slow things down. Yes, and while they are at it, they might as well sweep back the ocean with a broom.

To a certain extent, the recent cluelessness of banks has to do with expanding their size, computerizing the deposit and payments systems, and reducing the average branch bank to a single manager with either computers or new hires to help him. The information you need is available, but often in the home office a thousand miles away. Changes of this sort are hard to keep up with, and the bank officers dislike it, too. But the plaintive defense was recently given to a Committee of Congress, seen on television. "As long as the music keeps playing, we have to keep dancing."

Over in the investment banks, there are hundreds of very smart, very aggressive young fellows sitting at desks crowded together with three electronic monitors apiece, talking excitedly on the phones with their new best friends in foreign countries. Their job is not to know everything, but to know how to do something, and perform it very rapidly. Much of their knowledgeable talk is just bluffing; no one is sure what the other fellow knows. They all know the situation can't last; perhaps they can get promoted before some changed premise catches up with them. This isn't exactly greed, it's called high pressure. At any unexpected moment, that guy over in the corner office can come out and say, "You are all, all of you, fired as of this moment." It probably isn't his fault, either.

The fundamental situation is that depository institutions are being squeezed by technological change, and the blameless fact that investment banks can substitute their services at a lower cost because the money is accumulated by selling bonds in large denominations. The depository banks must try to accumulate deposits one by one in a recession, with interest rates held low for macroeconomic reasons dictated by the Federal Reserve. To level the playing field, depository banks have access to deposit insurance, which tempts them into high risk lending. Nobody can get hurt when it's all insured, Right? Every once in a while someone sends cold chills down the depository bank spine by calling for the abolition of deposit insurance, on the grounds that it promotes moral hazard. On the other hand, the investment banks are lobbying heavily to have deposit insurance extended to them, and they may well get it for their money market funds. This is all a pretty artificial controversy. The problem isn't evil, or deposit insurance, or being too big to fail. It's the nature of the struggle. Two different ways have been chosen to assemble capital. When one of them wins, the other knows it will die.

Let's not confuse this any further. The point of the discussion is to convey the immense pressure being placed on every minipixel of the financial system, by a gold rush taking advantage of the changes wrought by globalization of the world economy. Somewhere, a bubble will appear. It happened to be in real estate, as it often is in money panics. And if a bubble grows, somebody will pop it. Is it all his fault, too?

http://www.philadelphia-reflections.com/blog/2264.htm

Arbitration

The choice of "arbitration" as a term to describe a legal process seems a strange one, since it conflicts with the ordinary use of "arbitrary" as equivalent to a decision made without the use of logic or precedence, and even with "arbitrage" which implies slipping between the cracks. Nevertheless, frequent use of the terms seems to keep their meanings usably separate, at least in a city like Philadelphia which has a lot of lawyers. At any rate, when a lawyer who specializes in arbitration recently agreed to discuss the subject before a recent meeting of the Right Angle Club, the room had very few empty seats.

Arbitration

Arbitrage

Arbitration settles the same sort of dispute as damage suits, except there is no jury, and the decision of the Arbiter/Judge is final, without appeal. Most of the cases concern disputes between an individual and a corporation, where the two disputants have previously voluntarily decided to do business with each other, but had a falling out because of some misunderstanding. This puts the corporation in a position to insist on using arbitration in the event of a dispute, and the customer has accepted this condition as a requirement of doing business. Although it is true that an inclusion of such a requirement in a business contract is often unthinkingly accepted as part of a many-page fine-print boiler-plate provision, the requirement is so common it can often be regarded as well-understood. However, often it is not so well understood by a client, and a more serious criticism is that the company writes the detailed language, specifying who the arbitrator is to be.

Nevertheless, arbitration is cheaper and quicker than litigation, so the customer gets some real advantages from it, and the arbitrator generally is more expert in the subject matter than a random jury would be. In the event that a client is offered some choice of litigation in place of arbitration, he is often subjected to rather intense pressure to desist in the effort. Judges often quite openly admit they prefer a more rapid way to clear their calendar, and in the event of some technical complexity are even

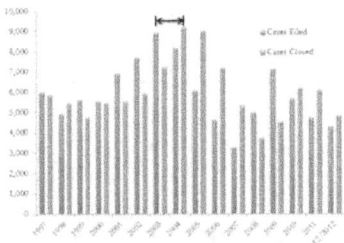

Abritration Cases

a little afraid to be drawn in over their heads by it. Right or wrong, when an arbitration decision is rendered, it is final. That is, there is no longer any danger a decision will be reversed on appeal. Most arbitration cases are disputes between investment broker/dealers, or commercial firms, and their clients, where the corporation has some hesitation in harming its commercial reputation by seeming to abuse clients. Therefore the situation tends to encourage a fair amount of brow-beating in order to get the client to sign some agreement that he has been satisfied.

In a sense, arbitration takes on the role of the Courts of Equity of an earlier era. A Court of Equity is designed to cope with a situation in which some obvious wrong exists, but no law exists to address it. As legislatures have had several centuries to pass legislation, Courts of

Equity have lacked much use; in fact, the current problem is probably that we have too much legislation. Therefore it is probably true that more important cases end up as litigation, while more routine or commercial cases congregate in arbitration. A random jury serves the purpose of speaking on behalf of Society in an area where the legislature has already had a chance to express the overall attitudes of Society; a jury speaks for fairness, as our civilization views fairness to be. Since an arbitration judge generally concentrates in a certain type of case, he generally is fairly expert in the law of the subject, and it seems likely he renders a better opinion of the law surrounding that particular topic. Whether he renders a better opinion of the merits of the case probably depends on whether his expertise has expanded with experience, or merely frozen with the passage of time.

Court of Equity

When the lecture was over, it was time for questions from the audience. It appears that club members were mainly entranced by the question of whether the choice of arbitration or litigation leads to a better outcome. In one way or another, the same question got the same cluster of answers: arbitration is cheaper, quicker and more final. But the questions kept getting re-phrased in different ways: is the outcome more or less fair than litigation? Finally, one old codger had the floor. "It seems to me, sir, that the plaintiff generally only has one case in a lifetime, whereas the defendant corporation may have thousands of cases. And the defendant gets to pick the arbitrator. Doesn't that seem to create an incentive for the arbitrator to favor the company which can send him more business?"

And the answer came quickly back, "Well, that's how it is. Just suck it up."

As the group filed out of the room, several members told the old codger, "Your question was better than the answer."

http://www.philadelphia-reflections.com/blog/2660.htm

Honoring the Fallen

The roarin' Twenties, just after the First World War, were a time when we seemed to change conventional attitudes about Society. But in many ways the convulsive changes of the Twenties were merely a process of facing up to what we already knew. In retrospect, many of the deeply emotional conflicts of that time, now seem entirely bearable. Scott Fitzgerald's most ponderous statement, the one that says "The test of a first-rate intelligence is the ability to hold two opposing ideas in mind at the same time and still retain the ability to function," reduces itself to the trivial agonies of loving two girls at a time, or choosing to stop smoking when you always knew you shouldn't start. Just about the only instance I can think of, where two deeply loved Philadelphia institutions are in seriously troubling conflict, are the First City

F. Scott Fitzgerald

Troop, and Quakerism. The matter came to mind at the Right Angle Club, when a Philadelphia Trooper who simply radiated the honorable dedications of upper-class Philadelphia gentlemen, meekly described his dedication to restoring the crumbling monuments of bravely fallen comrades. The monuments he finds and restores at great personal expense are not merely war heroes, although one suspects that is the root of it. The gravestones and monuments crumbling in the dust are markers of heroes of our civilization generally. But we do forget what we owe them, and neglect their monuments.

Although the dominant Quakers of Philadelphia's early days are now reduced to a handful of

Fourth Street Meeting House

practicing believers, almost every educated Philadelphian knows those beliefs pretty well. The early Friends did not even sympathize with carving their names on their tombstones. If you visit the Fourth Street Meetinghouse, you will be told that forty thousand bodies have been buried on the grounds, but only two graves have tombstones. The worship of grave markers, you will softly be told, is idolatry. The goal

of a funeral should not be to mourn a death, but to celebrate a life well-lived. And although the custom of gravestones has reasserted itself, it does not take long to be gently reminded that keeping alive the memories of one war's atrocities, can eventually lead to more wars. We recently have seen wars in Bosnia and Kosovo being fought over Thirteenth Century grievances which might better be forgotten. Some of this comes from immigration over three

Philadelphia First City Troop

thousand miles of ocean, but the effect is the same. I have no idea even what nationality my own 13th Century ancestors might have fought for, and I doubt if the world would be improved if I found out and sought to wreak vengeance for the inevitable atrocities.

But unless one is determined to denounce anything at all admirable about everything our society does to defend itself – and there are some who go that far – it is necessary to make a sad concession to force in successful governance. The 18th Century Quakers perhaps seldom acknowledged the need for occasional force as a condition for leadership, but they watched their children drift away from the religion, once they absorbed the lesson. Even those who choose conscientious objection for themselves, must occasionally acknowledge the debt they owe to those who do answer the call of force, and knowingly fail to survive it.

Society of Friends

There simply is no choice but to honor both sides of this issue, both permanently and side by side. There are some who can't, and in various ways fail to retain the ability to function. As in many of his more juvenile pronouncements, Fitzgerald does go much too far with assessing all the rest of Philadelphia as having less than first-rate intelligence. Philadelphians generally have at least a taste of the experience of holding

these two opposing ideas – the City Troop and the Society of Friends – in mind at the same time, with approval for both. And generally seeming somewhat improved for having made the struggle.

http://www.philadelphia-reflections.com/blog/2663.htm

The Last of the Algonquins

The Franklin Inn has trouble fitting fifty people in the audience, but it has a long history of members writing little plays for the special interest of its members. The latest was written by Jonathan Schau about Robert Benchley and Dorothy Parker, just before they went to Hollywood to try out, and received by the members with great merriment. Just in case anyone was still in doubt about the amount of alcohol being consumed in those days just after Repeal of Prohibition, I felt the urge to rise and tell the audience about an autopsy.

Jon Schau

Robert Benchley

In 1945 I was a sophomore medical student at Columbia's College of Physicians and Surgeons, taking the course in Pathology. With a perfectly straight face, Edith Sproul the professor of pathology introduced us to autopsy of a case of cirrhosis. The pathology classroom was not very different from the one at the University of Bologna which has been restored in Italy after unnamed pilots bombed the original into smithereens. But the famous painting of the original shows what it looked like, and the reproductions in Bologna and New York are very similar.

Nobody was indiscreet enough to mention it, but the canary-yellow subject on the table looked very much like Robert Benchley, whom the newspapers said had just died in that hospital. In any event, the subject had the worst looking case of cirrhosis of the liver which I ever hope to see. And in describing it I was surrounded by a club audience, every member of which had a glass in his hand. We don't need a cure for cirrhosis, of course. We have a cure for cirrhosis, perhaps a little more in use than it was in 1945, but not necessarily more popular.

While we are on the subject of the Algonquin Round Table, I might as well confess that my father-in-law was an occasional visitor. He wasn't an "official" member of the club, but **Algonquin Round Table** Alexander Woolcott had been his roommate at college, so he was welcome. Alexander was often in turn a visitor at what was my wife's house, and my mother-in-law absolutely detested what she called "a dirty old man", for reasons that were never explained to me. Alexander sprained his ankle while visiting, and it is family lore that the whole episode is central to the play called, "The Man Who Came to Dinner". In fairness to Alexander, I hope the play does as little justice to him, as it did to my mother-in-law.

http://www.philadelphia-reflections.com/blog/2667.htm

James F. Kilcur Esq.,

James F. Kilcur, 62, a labor lawyer who had been a top official at SEPTA, died Wednesday, Feb. 19, of leukemia at the Hospital of the University of Pennsylvania. The West Chester resident worked at SEPTA for 16 years, serving as general counsel and acting general manager.

He had been a partner at Saul Ewing since 1995, specializing in labor law and representing SEPTA management in labor negotiations.

"He gave you good advice and was a very steadying influence," said Pasquale "Pat" Deon Sr., chairman of the SEPTA board. "He was a great lawyer."

James F. Kilcur, Esq.

Mr. Kilcur was SEPTA's top lawyer in 1987, when he was selected to serve as general manager after the newly hired general manager, William Stead, abruptly quit after five weeks on the job. Stead, who had been hired from San Francisco's transit agency, became embroiled in a bitter struggle with suburban Republican members of the SEPTA board and resigned after he said he received a telephone death threat.

Mr. Kilcur, an unassuming, friendly man, brought a measure of calm to the rancorous SEPTA management for nearly a year during a nationwide search for a permanent replacement.

In 1988, SEPTA hired retired New Jersey Transportation Commissioner Louis Gambaccini as general manager, and Mr. Kilcur returned to the general counsel post.

"There was a lot of turmoil in the agency and at the board level at the time," said SEPTA's current general manager, Joseph Casey. "Jim was the right person for the job. . . . He handled all kinds of matters, and he treated everyone with respect.

"He was a very reasonable and fair individual," said Casey, adding that Mr. Kilcur's death "is hitting the SEPTA family pretty hard."

Even after leaving SEPTA in 1995, Mr. Kilcur remained active in the agency's labor negotiations, serving as a liaison to the SEPTA board. At Saul Ewing, he specialized in advising employers on labor issues, especially in the transportation and construction industries, said Fred Strober, a longtime colleague at the firm.

"He was an incredibly committed and focused person, who always remained calm and never got flustered, with a great sense of humor," Strober said. "He was the ultimate reasoned counselor."

Mr. Kilcur was born in Northeast Philadelphia to Rita and James Kilcur Sr. He was a varsity basketball player at Cardinal Dougherty High School, and he remained close to many of his grade school and high school friends for the rest of his life, his family said.

He was chairman of the board of trustees of his alma mater, DeSales University in Center Valley, at the time of his death. He received his law degree in 1977 from Widener University School of Law.

In the summer before his final year of law school, on June 5, 1976, Mr. Kilcur met his future wife, Maria Theresa Cheiffo, on the dance floor of the Bongo Room in Avalon.

"I was wearing a T-shirt with my name on it, and he came up and said, 'Hey, Terry, do you want to dance?' and I thought, 'How does he know my name?'" she recalled with a laugh Friday. "I forgot about the shirt."

They married in 1979.

Mr. Kilcur was active in the lives of his three sons, James III, Patrick, and Matthew. He coached their youth sports teams, advised them on career choices, and modeled an attitude of fairness and humility, they said Friday.

"He was very humble," James said. "He was a regular guy, he enjoyed his Scotch or beer, and could pretty much relate to anyone. He was never judgmental. And he could say a lot without talking a lot."

A devout Catholic, an avid golfer, and an active fund-raiser for the March of Dimes, he was also the Pennsylvania counsel for the Delaware Valley Regional Planning Commission.

In addition to his wife and sons, he is survived by his sister, Marguerite Eagan; a granddaughter; and two nephews.

A viewing will be held 7 to 9 p.m. Monday, Feb. 24, at St. Maximilian Kolbe Church, 300 Daly Dr., West Chester, and from 9 to 11 a.m. Tuesday at St. Mary Magdalen Church, 2430 N. Providence Rd., Media. A Funeral Mass will follow at St. Mary Magdalen.

Contributions may be made to DeSales University, 2755 Station Ave., Center Valley, Pa. 18034.

http://www.philadelphia-reflections.com/blog/2642.htm

Dr. F. Douglas Raymond Jr.

F. Douglas Raymond Jr., 88, a well-known Main Line rheumatologist and cofounder of the Bryn Mawr Rehabilitation Hospital, died Saturday, Oct. 18, of heart failure at Bryn Mawr Hospital, where he served for nearly four decades.

Dr. F. Douglas Raymond, Jr.

Born in Philadelphia, Dr. Raymond graduated from Episcopal Academy in 1944. He served in the Navy during World War II before returning to complete his education at Princeton University in 1950 and the University of Pennsylvania School of Medicine in 1954.

At Princeton, Dr. Raymond was a founding member of the a cappella singing group the Princeton Tigertones. A baritone, he later became a member of the Society for the Preservation and Encouragement of Barber Shop Quartet Singing in America, and sang with the Mainliners Chorus.

Dr. Raymond was an attending physician at Bryn Mawr Hospital for almost 40 years, and chief of rheumatology from 1965 to 1990. In the early years, he made house calls. He routinely took calls on weekends.

Recognizing the need for a space offering customized inpatient and outpatient rehabilitation programs, Dr. Raymond cofounded Bryn Mawr Rehab in 1966. The hospital in Malvern draws patients from throughout the mid-Atlantic region.

In 1969, responding to a perceived need for medical independence for doctors, he was one of six physicians to establish Bryn Mawr Medical Specialists Association.

The group comprising nearly 150 doctors in nine specialties was based at 933 Haverford Rd., but has moved to be nearer Bryn Mawr Hospital. Dr. Raymond, who was committed to educating the next generation of physicians, served on the faculties of Penn, Temple University Hospital and School of Medicine, and Jefferson Medical College.

After retiring from clinical practice in 1990, Dr. Raymond served for several years as medical director of Beaumont at Bryn Mawr, a retirement community.

"He helped set up the practice there before it even opened. He gave a physical to the first resident," said his wife, Carolyn MacReynolds Raymond.

Dr. Raymond was a fellow of the American College of Physicians and the Philadelphia College of Physicians, and was elected to the Alpha Omega Alpha Honor Medical Society in 1953.

He was a member of the Merion Cricket Club, the Nassau Club, and the Right Angle Club.

Dr. Raymond worshipped at the Church of the Redeemer in Bryn Mawr for most of his adult life. He served on the vestry at various times and founded the Men's Bible Study.

Surviving, besides his wife of 61 years, are sons Doug and David; daughters Ruth and Elizabeth Dougherty; and seven grandchildren.

A funeral service will be held at 1 p.m. Saturday, Nov. 1, at the Church of the Redeemer, 230 Pennswood Rd., Bryn Mawr, Pa. 19010. Interment is in the churchyard.

Contributions may be made to the Episcopal Academy Class of 1944 Fund, 1785 Bishop White Dr., Newtown Square, Pa. 19073, or to the Church of the Redeemer at the address above.

http://www.philadelphia-reflections.com/blog/2759.htm

Neale C. Bringhurst

NEALE C., 85 of Berwyn, PA died Saturday, November 29, 2014. A graduate of Harvard University in 1951, Harvard Business School in 1953 and The Union Institute with a Ph. D. in Psychology in 1993. He was past President of the Right Angle Club of Philadelphia, and Associate Member for over 30 years of the Orpheus Club of Philadelphia, a FINRA arbitrator and a professor at Immaculata University. He is survived by his daughters: Julia Lee and Amanda Carter and longtime companion Sheila Leith. Funeral Service will be held Saturday, December 6th, 11 A.M. at BRINGHURST FUNERAL HOME AT WEST LAUREL HILL CEMETERY, Bala Cynwyd, PA 19004. Interment is private. In lieu of flowers, contributions may be made to Philabundance.

Neale C. Bringhurst

http://www.philadelphia-reflections.com/blog/2760.htm

All poems copyright © Tom Howes unless otherwise indicated. Continued from pg 28

Hair Looms

Whereskin
Meets thin
Then guys
Seek guise
Must save
Each wave
In vain
Save mane

   First loops
   Next toupes
   Wear mops
   On tops
   Yet neat
   Heaps heat
   Locks swarm
   Wig warm

Heads Up

Look down
Coin found
This clue
Hooks you
Means luck
Has struck
Real wish
Catch fish

   So kneel
   Quick feel
   Prize looms
   Face blooms
   Hopes high
   Then sigh
   Why glum?
   Dad gum

Head Lines

Some hair
Stays there
From brim
To trim
Time's plow
Shapes brow
As dome
Nears chrome

   Male plan
   Mane man
   Seek highs
   Plugs dyes
   Hope sprouts
   Stand out
   Till grays
   Part ways

Iron Age

Seek job
Hob Nob
Dress Spiff
Pants stiff
Neat shirt
No dirt
Best sell
Look Well

   To pass
   Show class
   Top toes
   Trim clothes
   Pressed suit
   Bears fruit
   Self sold
   Join fold

Klutz Hit

Pros talk
Chat squawk
Love spew
Foul view
Sports plays
Few praise
Fore casts
Oft blasts

Last word
Fans heard
Their cash
Makes smash
These scores
Stun bores
Flip flops
Spin tops

Lap Tops

Cats sip
Then zip
Best bit
They sit
Sweet purr
Don't Stir
Make rounds
Soft sounds

Their choice
Your voice
Come near
Jump clear
This nap
Turns trap
Can't leave
Pets peeve

Line Up

Round pool
Young drool
Fish eyes
Hunt prize
Girls set
Drop net
Smiles looks
Cast hooks

Who'll tame
Wild game
All wait
As bait
Play loose
She's noose
Clothes taut
He's caught

Lost Cause

Phone pleas
Beg Please
New mails
Bring tales
With speed
Which one
Or none

We should
Do good
Yet scores
Breed more
So most
Are toast
When pled
For bread

Lost Cause

Phone pleas
Beg Please
New mails
Bring tales
With speed
Which one
Or none

    We should
    Do good
    Yet scores
    Breed more
    So most
    Are toast
    When pled
    For bread

Night Lite

New borns
Wake mourns
Their cries
Light skies
Each peep
Kills sleep
Hearts pound
Screams sounds

    Mom dad
    Both glad
    When shrill
    Turns still
    Queen's nest
    Praise rest
    Thank lord
    Lost chord

Pay Dirt

Fan mags
Oft rags
Snap pix
Sly tricks
They pry
You buy
New tells
Sin Sells

    Neath earth
    Much worth
    Rake muck
    Gold struck
    Flesh pots
    Were hot
    World's ways
    Grime pays

Poll Ticks

Vote time
Hopes climb
Loud voice
Chimes choice
Tight race
Keep pace
Count hours
Taste powers

    Charts trends
    Watch friends
    Hands spin
    Counts in
    Last click
    First pick!
    Room rocks
    Cleaned clocks

Pop's Art

Craft bloom
Dad's room
Paints splash
Slap dash
He's proud
Scenes loud
Works fast
Has blast

Crowds flock
Love shock
Praise jeer
Smirk sneer
Those smug
Shout hug
Rest hear
Daft ear

Psych Outs

Wind wails
Weird tales
Fans cheer
Love fear
Dark nights
Quick frights
Best part
Jump start

Ghouls ghosts
Best hosts
Get kicks
Scares tricks
These kooks
Seek spooks
Love taunts
Old haunts

Quick Steps

Born Wean
Tot Teen
School Grad
Wed Dad
Work Rounds
Ups Downs
Wife Bails
Hope Flails

Sweet Fate
New Mate
Wounds Mend
Jobs End
Song Fade
Dues Paid
Last Beat
Six Feet

Rack Ettes

Ten iz
Big biz
Crowds goes
Cheer pros
Watch verve
Each serve
Some rank
Then tank

Games go
To fro
Point set
Love let
Smash ace
Sets pace
Gross strain
Net gain

Red I

Take flight
Late night
Then reap
Less sleep
Dull drone
Aches bone
Comes morn
Never worn

Next day
You pay
Feel blue
Gray through
Last stop
Eyes pop
Face sags
Claims bags

Reign Checks

Realms flow
Kings go
Guile game
Stays same
Crowds cheer
Then jeer
Seek knights
End fight

Pawns shift
Crowns drift
Home rules
Rook fools
Queens play
Odds sway
Last state
Checks mate

Sole Mates

Shoe sale
Like grail
Fads in
Fem's sins
Must try
Then buy
Great styles
Huge piles

No lure
So sure
Makes gals
Life pals
Don't fight
This rite
You'll meet
Des feet

Our Jokemaster Has Another Side to Him

Haiku is an ancient Japanese form of poetry, originally in seventeen pieces. In recent years there has been a revival of haiku, usually shortened and omitting many of the symbolic rules. Tom Howes, a former president of the Right Angle Club, has his own version of the tradition, and has produced nearly a thousand of them, which Ross & Perry plans to publish.

Tom is better known to the club for his weekly joke presentation. The jokes seem entirely dissimilar, except it is obvious they follow certain rules. They come in threes, with the first a pun, then a short joke, and finally a whammo joke, to coin a phrase.

George Fisher, editor.

http://www.philadelphia-reflections.com/blog/2762.htm

www.ingramcontent.com/pod-product-compliance
Lightning Source LLC
Chambersburg PA
CBHW080544180626
46818CB00008B/3124